OMA AND THE PRINCE

A story about love, inner beauty, and going after your dreams.

WRITTEN BY SUSAN NGOZI NWOKEDI

ILLUSTRATED BY PAULA ADA CANTU

TopLine Productions & Entertainment, Co., LLC.

Published and distributed by TopLine Productions.

Special Appreciations and Dedications:

Special thanks to Paula A. Cantu for the countless hours she spent hand drawing the beautiful pictures that make up the illustrations of Oma and the Prince.

Special appreciation to my husband Kenenna, daughters Paula and Julia, my beautiful sister Ogo, and my students who shared their love of this story with me. Thank you for your love, time, support and feedback.

Most importantly, I give all the credit to God Almighty for the gift and love of writing.

This book is dedicated to my daughter Julia, who at the age of 3 years old asked me the question that inspired me to write Oma and the Prince. The question was "Am I a princess mommy?" "Yes, of course you are my love." I said, and then I looked at her nightgown and saw why she asked. Every little girl is a princess.

Oma and the Prince is a story about true love, inner beauty, and going after your dreams.

Once upon a time, in a beautiful kingdom in West Africa, lived a young prince.

The prince was of age to marry. His father, King Ike, invited every young girl of marrying age from the kingdom and the neighboring villages to a feast at the palace so that the prince could choose his future wife.

Every royal and elite girl of age traveled to the feast. The prince did not like any of the girls because they were shallow, spoiled, and fake. But he had to get married to produce an heir to the throne.

Meanwhile, in a nearby village, with palm trees, little mud huts, and a narrow dirt road that led to a beautiful stream, was a young girl named Oma. She spent most of her day going to the stream to fetch water, working on her family's tiny garden and helping her mother sell the little produce they harvested from their garden at the market.

She was very friendly, smiled a lot, and even hummed a tune as she completed her daily chores. She was an only child and her parents loved her dearly.

Oma was born with a rare skin disease. The disease left her face covered with large boils and scars. Other children teased and made fun of her.

Oma and her family were very poor. They lived in one of the little mud huts. From day to day, they got by only on bread and the few fish her father caught from the river.

During the summer months, when water was scarce, Oma took water to the elders of the village. They loved and blessed her.

Back at the palace, the king and queen were very worried because the prince, their only child, had not yet picked a wife.

If he did not marry and produce an heir, the king's evil cousin would take the throne and disaster would befall the kingdom.

You see, many years ago, the gods had placed a curse on the evil cousin's great-great-grandfather and his future generations.

The story is, the great-great-grandfather killed an innocent child as a sacrificial offering to the devil. He also sold his own soul to the devil for godlike powers.

To punish him for his evil deeds, he and his future

generations were cursed. One consequence of the curse

was losing his rights to the throne. His younger brother,

king Ike's great grandfather, was given the throne instead.

The second consequence of the curse was: should any of the evil brother's offspring take the throne, the entire kingdom would be doomed and everyone would be banished because of the curse.

The king was troubled by this fearsome curse, so he begged his son to marry one of the girls he had seen at the feast. But the prince said, "No, father, I did not see my wife there."

Oma's circumstance, meanwhile, had grown worse. Her skin disease had spread to other parts of her body.

One night, Oma dreamt that she was meeting the prince at the palace.

She awoke and told her mother about the dream. A big smile ran across her mother's face. She quickly lost her smile as she remembered it was only a dream. After all, the chances of her daughter meeting and marrying the prince were hopeless. This made her sad, so she told Oma not to talk about her dreams.

Oma's dreams about the prince continued. Since her mother could not change her mind or stop her from dreaming, Oma's mother decided to share her daughter's dream with others in the village. They all made fun of Oma and laughed at her. One of them said, "Imagine the nerves of that ugly child, dreaming about the prince." Their mean words and mockery did not stop Oma.

One day, Oma said to her mother, "Mama, in my dreams about the prince, I am whole. I have no scars, no boils, and nothing ugly at all." "Mama, I am beautiful in this dream, and I am the prince's wife. Mama, I am a princess in the dream."

Oma's mom listened and saw how happy her daughter looked as she talked about her dreams. "My daughter," she said, "I'll talk to your Papa tomorrow. If he says yes, we will take you to the palace to meet the prince." Oma was so excited! "Oh, Mama" she said, "thank you, thank you so much!"

That night, Oma's mother talked to her husband about their daughter's dreams and her requests to meet the prince.

"Mama Oma," said the father, "do you know what you are saying?" "Look at us: we are very poor, and Oma's condition has disfigured her for life and has put many obstacles in her way."

"Oh, Papa Oma," said the mother, "I understand your worries, but you know your daughter. She is a very good girl with the most beautiful heart. She is very sincere, and she is sure of herself. If she has these dreams, we cannot stop her from following them. I don't think we can do any harm by showing our support and love to our daughter." Oma's father nodded his head in agreement.

The next day, Oma and her parents set off on foot to travel to the palace. On the way, some villagers tried to change their minds. They teased, booed and even spat on them.

One angry woman yelled, "Look at you: an ugly duckling reaching for a prince when my beautiful Ada did not even stand a chance." Oma and her parents did not stop. They kept their eyes fixed on the palace.

They arrived at the palace but were not allowed through the gates. Oma fell on her knees to beg. "Get up, child," said the head guard. "It must be very important for you to see the king and queen." He signaled to another guard to take the family to see the king and queen at once.

When the queen saw Oma, she turned her nose up at her and said, "Is this a jest? Young lady, what do you think you are doing here?" Oma replied in her soft and respectful manner: "My queen, I am here to see the prince."

The king looked up at her in shock. The queen said, "I am so sorry to disappoint you, my dear child, but you are not the kind of girl my son seeks." "Why, you are so ugly! And looking at you and your parents, you are poorer than my servants."

Just as the queen finished talking, the prince entered the palace. His eyes locked with Oma's eyes, and time froze. "This is my wife," said the prince.

The queen fainted, and the king bolted from his throne. "Son," said the king, "have you lost your mind? This girl cannot be your wife. She is disfigured and poor. Your wife must be beautiful and rich." The prince said, "She is my choice, Father."

Oma was not surprised. She had believed all along that the prince had been dreaming of her. She had known her heart and faith would not fail her.

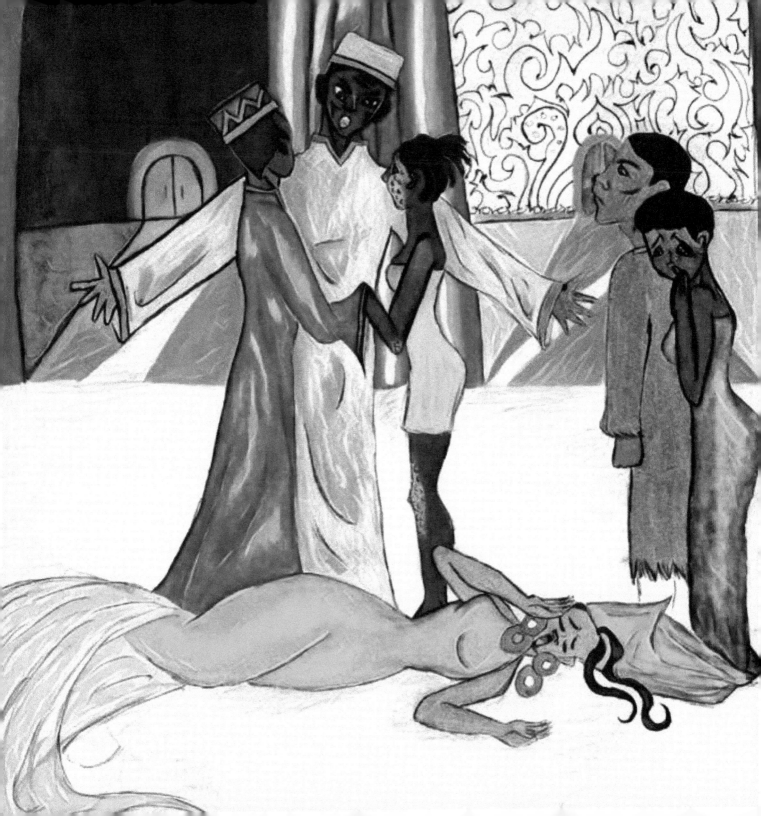

"Father," said the prince. "If I don't marry Oma, I will not marry at all." The queen, who was recovering from her faint, broke down again.

Her parents were shocked. Her mother began to cry.

Oma's parents had never mentioned her name since entering the palace. Yet, the prince called her by name.

The king and queen could not change their son's mind. The prince told his parents he had been dreaming about Oma for as long as he could remember. "Oma is the most beautiful girl I have ever seen. She has a pure and beautiful heart," said the prince. He told his parents he had known that faith would bring them together.

He also told them that Oma's kind heart was the only thing that could break the curse pronounced on his evil cousin.

When the king heard this, he supported his son's choice to marry Oma. Oma and her parents were invited to stay at the palace. The queen too supported her son, but she still turned up her nose at Oma and her parents.

Everyone in the kingdom and Oma's village was invited to the wedding. People were shocked. Some even gossiped that Oma and her family had used voodoo to win the prince over.

Oma's attendants were not kind to her at first. But they quickly fell in love with her because she was truly beautiful on the inside.

One day, while in the garden with the prince, Oma told him of her desire to be beautiful on their wedding day. "My prince," she said, "I want to be whole. I want to look beautiful on our wedding day." "My beauty," said the prince, "you are very beautiful already." "I love you just the way you are. You are whole to me."

"Oh, my prince," said Oma, "but in my dreams, I saw myself without scars and blotches. My skin was smooth and beautiful." "I want to look the same way on our wedding day."

So, the prince said, "My beauty, I will talk to the royal doctor. He should have a cure; he has a cure for everything."

After the royal doctor had looked at Oma's skin, he told the prince that her condition was very easy to treat. The only reason Oma had been suffering from this disease all her life was that her parents were too poor to take her to the doctor.

Oma's skin disease was cured, and she became the most beautiful girl in all kingdoms throughout the country. No one except Oma, the prince, and the royal doctor knew she had been cured.

So, on the wedding day, when the prince removed her veil to kiss her, everyone was shocked to see how beautiful she looked. Her skin was so smooth that it sparkled.

Everyone was so happy. The elders from her village were happy and very proud of her. "Look at our little Oma, now a princess," said one of them.

Her parents were so proud. They had always been proud of her, but especially because she held on to her dreams. She did not let anything or anyone take her dreams away from her.

Oma and the prince were married. They had three sons and two daughters.

The kingdom became the richest kingdom of all time in the country. The king and queen were happy, and they loved Oma and her family.

The curse on the evil cousin was broken, and he became the most noted right-hand man to the prince. It turned out that the only way the curse could be broken was if any member of the royal family married for love. Though Oma was a poor, ugly girl with disfigured face, the prince loved her. Because of his love for her, the curse was broken.

And they all lived happily ever after.

The End

CPSIA information can be obtained
at www.ICGtesting.com
Printed in the USA
BVHW021147190721
612318BV00013B/181

9 780578 592923